A GIFT FOR:

....

....

THE TALE OF
YOU

Hopping
into Life

FREDERICK WARNE
Penguin Young Readers Group
An Imprint of Penguin Random House LLC

Penguin supports copyright. Copyright fuels creativity, encourages diverse voices, promotes free speech, and creates a vibrant culture. Thank you for buying an authorized edition of this book and for complying with copyright laws by not reproducing, scanning, or distributing any part of it in any form without permission. You are supporting writers and allowing Penguin to continue to publish books for every reader.

Illustrations first published in *The Tale of Peter Rabbit* by Frederick Warne 1902
New reproductions of Beatrix Potter's illustrations first published 2002
Color reproduction by EAE Creative Colour Ltd, Norwich, England

www.peterrabbit.com

Published in 2016 by Frederick Warne, an imprint of Penguin Random House LLC, 345 Hudson Street, New York, New York 10014

Manufactured in China

ISBN 978–0–14–136384–4

10 9 8 7 6 5 4 3 2 1

THE TALE OF
YOU

TM

Hopping
into Life

Based on *The Tale of Peter Rabbit* by
BEATRIX POTTER

Now
that you are fully grown,
it is time
for you to set off on
your own.

So
run along,
my little bunny,
and don't get into
mischief!

Make sure
you stop to gather all
the sweet things
life will offer
you.

Then
take a chance,
squeeze under the gate, and
discover somewhere
new.

A nibble here,
a nibble there –
make sure you taste life
to the fullest!

Just remember
you can have
too much of a
good thing.

You never know
who
you might meet
around the
corner…

Not everyone
is a **friend** –
you might need to be
quick on your
feet!

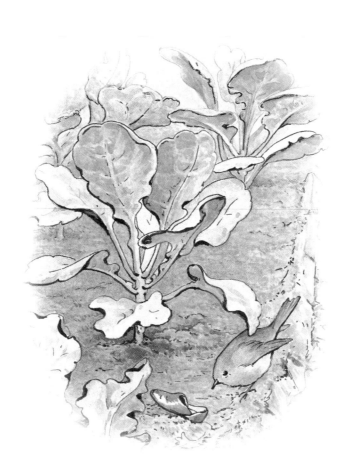

Sometimes
you may
lose
your way.

And sometimes
life may catch **you**
by **surprise**.

It's
all right to cry –
but **don't**
give up.

Take a deep breath,
summon your
courage, and
wriggle free!

And if you need
to **hide away**
for a bit, then **do**.

Hold tight, until you're
ready to **face**
the world **again**.

You'll **arrive** at
many **doors** –
some **open** and
some **closed**.

No matter
what happens,
I know you'll find
your way.

And if
you **ever** long
to come **home,**
I will be **there** . . .

. . .with warm food,
a **listening ear**
and a **cozy** bed . . .

. . . until you're
ready for your
next **great**
adventure!